"Ten seconds?" roared the anchorman to his
camera operator. "Ten seconds?
Why didn't you say so? My wire showing?
Is my suit straight? Hair all right? ..."
The cameraman counted down and pointed at the
anchorman as the camera light came on.

The anchorman, suddenly cool and collected,
looked straight into the camera. "Hello," he said.
"This is Dan Splatter with the Six O'clock Ooze
News. Today's big story . . ."

With a huge bang and a puff of smoke,
Beetlejuice popped onto the news desk.
"Stop the presses," he shouted into the camera.

"Huh?" asked a confused Splatter.

"Tonight's top story," said Beetlejuice, leaning
toward the camera, "is . . .

Beetlejuice for President!"

Books by B. J. Specter

Beetlejuice #1: Beetlejuice for President
Beetlejuice #2: Lydia's Scream Date
Beetlejuice #3: Rock 'N' Roll Nightmare
Beetlejuice #4: Twisted Tours
Beetlejuice #5: Camp Fright

Available from MINSTREL Books

BEETLEJUICE
FOR PRESIDENT

B.J. Specter

Illustrated by Ernesto Colón

A MINSTREL® BOOK

PUBLISHED BY POCKET BOOKS

New York   London   Toronto   Sydney   Tokyo   Singapore

For Luana

This book is a work of fiction. Names, characters, places and incidents are either the product of the author's imagination or are used fictitiously. Any resemblance to actual events or locales or persons, living or dead, is entirely coincidental.

A MINSTREL PAPERBACK *ORIGINAL*

A Minstrel Book published by
POCKET BOOKS, a division of Simon & Schuster Inc.
1230 Avenue of the Americas, New York NY 10020

Copyright © 1992 by The Geffen Film Company.
BEETLEJUICE, characters, names and all related indicia are trademarks of
The Geffen Film Company © 1992.

ISBN: 0-671-75552-8

First Minstrel Books printing February 1992

10   9   8   7   6   5   4   3   2

A MINSTREL BOOK and colophon are registered trademarks of Simon & Schuster Inc.

Printed in U.S.A.

Creative Media Applications
Book series developed by Dan Oehlsen, Lary Rosenblatt & Barbara Stewart
Art direction by Fred Gates Design
Cover painting by Greg Wray
Interior Illustrations by Ernesto Colón
Edited by Lucy Rosendahl

Special thanks to Ruth Ashby, Lisa Clancy, Gina Bonanno, Karen McTier, Rand Brenner, and Laurie Pessell.

CHAPTER ONE

FIT TO BE TIED

LYDIA DEETZ trudged up the front steps of her house. "What a boring day," she moaned. "Nothing's ever new in Peaceful Pines. This town was born old." She pushed open the front door with a sigh.

A blinding light hit her eyes. A shrill whistle pierced the air. The house shook. Dust whirled in small tornadoes all around the floor as a huge, striped locomotive raced down the stairs, heading straight for Lydia.

Lydia rolled her eyes. "Beetlejuice," she said.

The locomotive flipped head-over-wheels and turned into a mischievous ghoul with yellow hair, purplish skin, green rotting teeth, and tattered clothes. The ghoul slammed into a wall, then bounced to his feet. "Ta-dah!" he yelled, throwing out his arms. Then, clutching his sides, he collapsed to the floor in a fit of laughter.

Lydia rolled her eyes and tried not to laugh herself.

She actually looked forward to Beetlejuice greeting her in strange ways when she came home. His antics were always welcome after a long, dull day at Miss Shannon's School for Girls. As far as Lydia was concerned, Beetlejuice made her house the one bright spot, or maybe dark spot, in all of Peaceful Pines.

"You shouldn't make so much noise," Lydia said. "My parents might come to investigate."

"Don't worry, babes," said Beetlejuice, picking a bug from between his teeth. "Charles is the only one inside, and he's watching television."

Lydia laughed. When her dad, Charles, was in front of the television, nothing disturbed him.

"I'll tell you, Lyds," Beetlejuice continued, "I know I seem a bit wild." Hair began sprouting from his face, as he changed to a wild beast. "But I need a release of some sort." Steam shot out of his ears. "I mean, being a ghost used to be a blast. Now I can't find a soul with any afterlife in it. It's hard to find a ghoul who measures down to yours truly, the ghost with the most. It's lonely at the bottom, Lyds."

6

Lydia giggled. "Well, just stick with me, Beetlejuice. We'll find some fun in one of these boring old worlds—mine or yours."

"I'm with you, babes," said Beetlejuice as he balled himself up into a wad of gum on her shoe.

"Beetlejuice!" Lydia complained, trying to scrape him off her shoe. "Stick with me, not on me!" Lydia's black shoes were the only thing she liked about her school uniform. At home, Lydia normally wore nothing but black. Black tights, black T-shirt and leggings, black cape. Miss Shannon's School for Girls, though, made her wear a boring red plaid uniform. She improved this outfit with her own spider pin, bat-shaped barrettes, and tarantula necklace.

A loud banging captured their attention. "Yikes!," yelled Beetlejuice, leaping into Lydia's arms.

Bang! Bang! Bang! The noise came from outside.

"Frightened, babes?" asked Beetlejuice.

Lydia dropped Beetlejuice and went to look out the window. "Delia's in the backyard," said Lydia. Delia was Lydia's stepmother. She had developed many peculiar ways of showing how much she missed living in the city since the family moved to Peaceful Pines a year ago. Lydia didn't much care where they lived. But if they hadn't moved she would never have met Beetlejuice. He haunted her room and had become her best friend.

7

"What's she doing?" asked Beetlejuice.

"I don't really know," Lydia confessed.

"Oh, to be a fly on the wall inside her head," Beetlejuice mused, sprouting huge antennae, bug eyes, and lacy wings. He shrunk down to a tiny size and landed with a buzzing noise on Lydia's nose. "There's got to be plenty of room there."

"But her head's so thick," giggled Lydia, looking cross-eyed at the black-and-white shaped fly. "It's probably pretty hard to get inside. Let's find out what she's up to."

She blew Beetlejuice off the tip of her nose. He flipped back into his normal size and shape and smacked his fist into his palm. "Hey, Lyds," he declared. "I'll come along in disguise." Beetlejuice made it a point not to let Lydia's parents see him.

"What kind of disguise?" asked Lydia.

"I don't know," said Beetlejuice. "I'll have to stretch my imagination." He grabbed his ears and pulled until his head was three feet wide and three inches high. Then he let go. His head slapped back together. "Got it!" he cried, shrinking himself very small. "I'll go as your hairband!"

Lydia loved the idea. She grabbed Beetlejuice and wrapped him around the shaft of hair that stuck straight up from her head. Then she went outside.

Delia Deetz was humming while she hammered. *Bang! Bang! Bang!* A pile of wood, many sheets of cardboard, and some cans of paint were at her feet. Not the things Delia normally hammered. Those things—the old wooden blocks, wire, tin cans and the like—were strewn about the yard. Delia considered herself a sculptor, though all of her odd contraptions were either falling apart in the yard or gathering dust in the attic.

"What's this?" asked Lydia. "Sign sculpture?"

"Hmm?" said Delia, turning around. "Oh, Lydia. No, of course not. I'm making campaign signs."

"What are you campaigning for?" Lydia asked.

"Oh, they're not for me," Delia replied. "They're for your father. He's running for town council."

Lydia scratched her head. "Does he know this?"

"I've told him," said Delia.

"You mean ordered him," Beetlejuice said under his breath.

Delia gave Lydia a suspicious look. "What was that, dear? Your voice sounded kind of funny."

"Sorry," said Lydia, clearing her throat. "I've got a frog in my throat."

"Ribbit," croaked Beetlejuice. He turned himself into a frog and jumped off Lydia's head. With the hairband gone, Lydia's hair fell down over her face.

"I was talking to Nadine Hemlock of the Sugar Maple Society," said Delia, "and she said it was important to get someone on the town council who would keep developers from building too much in our quaint little town. Since your father has dragged us all to live here in Peaceful Pines, he might as well make a contribution."

"But Mom," said Lydia, brushing the hair out of her eyes. "Since when have you cared about developers and Peaceful Pines?"

"Ribbit, ribbit," Beetlejuice croaked happily. He jumped around Delia's and Lydia's feet.

Delia seemed not to have heard him or Lydia. "And it so happens," she continued, "that the town council is also considering putting a new sculpture in the town square. Don't you just think Charles would be the perfect person to choose a sculptor?"

"Oh no," moaned Lydia. Now she understood. Delia didn't care about developers. She wanted Charles on the town council to make sure they chose one of her sculptures to display.

Beetlejuice was croaking louder now, trying to draw attention to himself. "Ribbit!" he said. He jumped. "Ribbit!" Then he froze. He may not have managed to capture Delia's attention, but he had been noticed by a cat prowling the edge of the backyard. "Oops," said Beetlejuice.

The cat dashed toward him. "RIBBIT!" Beetlejuice croaked. He started hopping madly.

Lydia heard the commotion and looked around, trying to figure out what was happening. Delia just hummed and hammered her signs.

The cat sprinted between Lydia's legs. Beetlejuice leapt onto Delia's shoulder, and Delia shrieked. The cat lunged after Beetlejuice, but Delia swatted at it, flinging the cat in one direction and Beetlejuice in the other. He fell straight into the bucket of paint, splashing color all over Delia's campaign signs.

"Oh no!" Lydia cried, realizing what was happening. She reached into the paint bucket and pulled Beetlejuice out.

"Shoo," Delia shouted at the cat, chasing it away. Then she turned around.

Lydia was standing over the bucket, her hand still dripping. The campaign signs were all spotted with paint. "Lydia!" cried Delia. "What have you done?"

Lydia whipped her hands behind her back, hiding Beetlejuice the frog.

"I worked so hard on these campaign signs," pouted Delia. "Now you've ruined them!"

Lydia thought fast. "I was just . . . uh . . . decorating them," she said. "You know, you want your signs to stand out from all the others."

"But they have big spots on them!" shrieked Delia, waving her hands in the air.

"Exactly!" Lydia agreed. "And this can be your campaign slogan: *It's easy to spot the right candidate: Charles Deetz.*"

Delia stopped shrieking and clapped her hands together. "Why, Lydia. That's wonderful. I'm so happy you're helping me." She snatched up the paint bucket. "Maybe just a few more spots, then."

"Uh," Lydia said, "I've really got to get to my homework." She hurried back into the house, still holding Beetlejuice behind her back.

As soon as they were inside, Beetlejuice returned to his normal shape. "Boy, what a laugh," he said. "Charles running for office."

"Why is that such a laugh?" she asked, defending her father.

"People want strong leaders," said Beetlejuice, his biceps pumping up. "They want dynamic, active, flashy leaders." He began to flash and blink like a neon sign.

"That's not true," said Lydia. "What people really care about is what a candidate stands for. Charles loves Peaceful Pines. He wouldn't let any developers destroy it."

She ran up the stairs to her room.

"Hey Lyds," said Beetlejuice, following her to her room. "People want someone like me!"

Lydia giggled. "Like you? Beetlejuice," she said, "you can't run for our town council."

"Who said anything about that?" replied Beetlejuice. He was so excited, he was floating in the middle of Lydia's room. "I'm talking about running for . . . President of the Neitherworld!"

"Does the Neitherworld have a president?" Lydia asked.

"Not yet," said Beetlejuice. "But so what? I'm perfect for the job. I'm a born politician. I'm charming. A real cool ghoul. I can bring some spirit, some spark, some electricity to the place. And, hey, I'll become a celebrity!"

"Beetlejuice, you're impossible," said Lydia.

"But here it is, babes. You think Peaceful Pines is boring? You haven't been to the Neitherworld lately. Let me tell you, Delia—no, even Charles would find it boring. So I'm running on the Fun Platform—a good time in the afterlife. So come on, babes. Let's get to it." He was bursting with excitement. "Zap us to the Neitherworld."

This was an invitation Lydia could never resist. "Beetlejuice, Beetlejuice, Beetlejuice!" she cried. And with a burst of lightning and a crack of thunder, they disappeared.

CHAPTER TWO

THE CAMPAIGN OF IT ALL

LYDIA tumbled onto the hard, rocky ground of the Neitherworld. "Ugh," she said, shaking her head. "I wish I could just snap my fingers instead."

As she got to her feet, a poster as high as a building began unrolling itself. A huge picture of Beetlejuice beamed out at the bleak Neitherworld landscape. "BEETLEJUICE FOR PRESIDENT," read the poster in black-and-white striped letters.

Then something funny happened. The poster winked at her. "What do you think, Lyds?" asked the huge, flattened face.

"Beetlejuice!" Lydia cried, delighted.

But suddenly his face started trembling. A look of panic crossed his eyes. "Ahhh," screamed Beetlejuice, and the whole poster crashed down. The force of the collapse sent Lydia tumbling.

"Sorry, babes," Beetlejuice said, picking himself up off the ground. "I can't keep those tall tales up for long. It's too much of a stretch."

"That's okay," Lydia said. "I know you get too big for your britches sometimes."

The two of them walked toward Beetlejuice's house, which was perched on the edge of a cliff, at the end of the main road leading out of the Neitherworld. The Roadhouse was a shabby building that was falling to pieces. It was part junkyard, part boardinghouse, part circus. Beetlejuice lived there with a few other ghouls.

"So begins my great campaign," declared Beetlejuice as he bounded up the rickety front steps. The knocker came off in his hands as he reached up to bang on the door.

"Knock knock," the knocker said in a raspy voice.

"Who's there?" Beetlejuice exclaimed.

"The Pain."

"The Pain who?" Beetlejuice inquired.

"The Campaign of it all!" The door knocker laughed and clacked his knocker loudly.

The door opened, and Lydia and Beetlejuice went into the Roadhouse.

"So we know your platform . . ." said Lydia, as Beetlejuice transformed himself into a stage with a podium on it. "Be serious, Beetlejuice. You need a plan to win a presidential election."

"Election?" he howled, snapping back to his former shape. "What election?"

"That's how you get to be president," Lydia explained. "You hold an election and people vote for you. You campaign to get people's votes. What did you think the campaign was about?"

"I figured I'd just tell people the news." Beetlejuice frowned. "But this changes everything. Now I'd better put on my thinking cap." He held out his hand, and a cap popped into it.

"No, no," Beetlejuice grumbled, batting the cap away with his other hand. "That's my golfing cap. I need my thinking cap."

Another cap appeared his hand.

Swat! "Not my yachting cap," Beetlejuice said. Pop! "Not my bus driver's cap . . . not my hubcap . . . not my polo helmet . . . not my hard hat . . . not my bottle cap . . . not my ten gallon . . ." Hats and caps of all sizes and shapes kept popping into one hand. Beetlejuice kept batting them aside with the other.

"Stop," cried Lydia. She was nearly buried beneath a pile of hats. "Beetlejuice, you've got to find a different way to think."

"You're right, babes," said Beetlejuice. He whacked the end of his nose, sending his head spinning round and round. "I've just got to get my head screwed on right."

"Look," said Lydia. "Why don't you just start with Jacques and Ginger in the Roadhouse?"

"Hey, babes. That's just what I had in mind." Beetlejuice straightened up and went into the Roadhouse. At the first door he turned his hand into a hammer and gave a few bangs.

Jacques La Lean, the weight-lifting skeleton, opened the door. He wore his usual shorts and half T-shirt, which showed off the bottom of his ribcage. His skull was capped with a beret, and V- shaped eyebrows and a thin mustache framed the bones of his face.

"Wot do you want?" Jacques asked in his French accent. He didn't look happy to see Beetlejuice.

"Ahem!" Beetlejuice cleared his throat. "How do you do, Jacques?"

"Keep eet short, Byetelzhooze," said Jacques, shaking a dumbbell at him. "I'm workeeng out."

"Just wanted to mention," said Beetlejuice, "I'm running for president of the Neitherworld. This place has gotten too serious, too intense. As president I'm going to bring the fun back. I'm sure I can count on your vote on election day."

"Zoot!" Jacques exclaimed. He slammed the door so hard the wall shook. Startled, a bunch of bugs crawled out of the cracks in the wall and started scurrying about. Beetlejuice grabbed a bug and swallowed it.

18

Lydia giggled and slapped Beetlejuice on the back. "Way to go, Beetlejuice," she said. "Looks like you've convinced Jacques."

"Minor setback," Beetlejuice assured her. He produced an admiral's cap on his head. "I've not yet begun to fight."

His hand became a jackhammer. He thumped on Jacques's door. The force of his pounding shook loose a chunk of the ceiling. It fell on Beetlejuice's head.

"Ow!" yelped Beetlejuice.

Jacques flung the door open. "Stop this jokeeng, Byetelzhooze!" he cried. "Ze Neitherworld has no president!"

"Not yet," Beetlejuice corrected him. "But all we need is a little election. Think of it!"

Jacques began to close the door again, but Beetlejuice held it open.

"Look at us, Jacques. This is the Neitherworld. We can do whatever we want to, and we're not doing anything. Ghouls and goblins and skeletons and bats and spiders just wander about the Shocking Mall or sit around watching television. We might as well be normal.

"Think of it!" Beetlejuice exclaimed. He flung his arms wide. "We need disorganization." He turned his body into a file cabinet and thumbed through the folders. They were labeled "Heart," "Lungs," "Stomach," "Liver." In each folder was the correct organ. "Enough of a place for everything and everything in its place."

"I like things as they are," said Jacques.

"Loosen up!" Beetlejuice bellowed. "Let things go!" He flung the folders across the room. His body fell to pieces. "Let things get out of control," his head added, bouncing up and down. His arms danced with his legs, fingers snapped, toes tapped, all his parts twisted and spun.

Beetlejuice's head let out an ear-splitting whistle and his body parts flew back together. "As the president, I can make things happen," he said. "I can bring chaos where there's order. I can bring excitement where there's boredom. I can make the afterlife worth dying for!"

"But how does Byetelzhooze know what I want?" Jacques protested.

"Listen to me, Jacques," said Beetlejuice, dashing over to the skeleton. He threw his arm around Jacques's bony shoulder blades. "Imagine this. If I'm elected president, I'll make everybody exercise an hour a day."

"Oh," Jacques mused. "Zat would be nice."

"No more couch potatoes." Beetlejuice turned into a huge potato. "Not only that," Beetlejuice added, "but from now on, everyone speaks French."

20

"Impossible!"

"Moi assurez-vous, babes," said Beetlejuice. "You just have to get me elected."

"Beetlejuice!" Lydia cried. "You can't do that."

"Ignore the girl in the black dress," Beetlejuice said smoothly.

"Hmm," Jacques said. "I like this idea."

"Think it over, Jacques," Beetlejuice said. "Meanwhile, I've got to split. Oops. I mean," he added, "I've got to move on." But half of him already had.

Lydia and both halves of Beetlejuice's body walked toward Ginger's door. "I think I'm getting the hang of this stuff," Beetlejuice told Lydia.

"But Beetlejuice," said Lydia. "How can you possibly make everyone speak French?"

"I'll worry about that later," said Beetlejuice. "After I'm elected. Now, let's see how I do with the tap-dancing spider." Pulling himself together, he knocked crisply on Ginger's door.

The sound of tapping feet, lots of them, got closer and closer. Beetlejuice spotted a fly buzzing near the wall. He flicked out his long, striped tongue and nabbed it. He picked the fly off his tongue. "Give the spiders what they want," he chuckled.

Ginger opened her door. She was a short spider with wide eyes. She wore too much lipstick, trying to look glamorous. "Beetlejuice," she squealed. "I'm glad you're here. Wait till you see my new dance!"

"My lady," sang Beetlejuice, bowing low and presenting Ginger with the fly.

Ginger frowned and crossed two of her eight legs. "What's wrong with it?" she asked.

"I'm truly hurt," said Beetlejuice. "How could you think there was something wrong with it?"

"Well," Ginger replied, "the last fly you gave me was a super-compressed sponge. My stomach ached for a week. The fly before that was your Super-Duper Bug Zapper."

"Oh yeah," Beetlejuice said. "I got a charge out of that."

"So did I," Ginger said icily.

Beetlejuice popped the fly into his mouth and swallowed. "Let me get right to the point," he said. "I'm running for president of the Neitherworld, and I need your vote."

"Why would I vote for you?"

Beetlejuice fell to his knees so he could drape his arm over Ginger's back. "Listen, babes," he said. "If I'm elected president, I'll see to it that all shoes come in groups of eight, not just in pairs."

Ginger's eyes widened. "Oh my!"

"With taps on them," Beetlejuice added with a smile.

"Goodness!"

"Yeah," Beetlejuice rattled on. "I want to bring some pizzazz back to the afterlife. And where better to begin than with bugs! I promise a fly in every web. And for you, babes, two flies!"

Ginger gasped with delight.

Suddenly a Texas-twanged voice boomed out from behind them. "What's this about y'all talking French?"

Beetlejuice and Lydia whirled around. A scary face under a hulking ball of hair with a cowboy hat perched on top stood facing them. "It's the Monster from Across the Street," Lydia gasped.

"And his dog Poopsie," moaned Beetlejuice, as the ugly, horned pug stepped out from behind the Monster.

"That crazy ol' French skeleton just came running past my door," said the Monster. "Claiming that Beetlejuice is saying everyone's gotta talk French. Well not me, buster. Not on your afterlife!"

"Er . . . um . . ." said Beetlejuice. "French poodles. Talking French poodles, is what I said." Beetlejuice's hair turned into a huge curly puff. His ears got curly and floppy. He sprouted a tail.

Poopsie perked up his ears.

"I was talking about shipping a few French poodles into the Neitherworld," continued Beetlejuice, "to be pals for all the nice dogs here."

The Monster looked down at his dog. "You like French poodles, Poopsie?" he asked.

Poopsie snarled in excitement.

"Sure he does," said Beetlejuice, wagging his own tail. "So all you've got to do is vote for me on election day."

A few minutes later, Beetlejuice, back to his ghoulish self, and Lydia left the Roadhouse. They left Ginger and the Monster talking excitedly about the new president.

"Things are really taking off," Beetlejuice said to Lydia. "This will be a piece of cake." He turned into a wedge, his head covered with frosting.

Lydia dipped her hand in the frosting. "If you're not careful with your promises," she said, "things could get a bit sticky."

"Nothing to worry about, Lyds," Beetlejuice said, grinning. "Now, you know what this campaign needs?"

"What?"

Beetlejuice gave her a sly smile. "Television coverage!" A huge television appeared above his head and then dropped, squashing him flat.

CHAPTER THREE

DRIBBLING RIVALRY

"TEN SECONDS?" roared the anchorman to his camera operator. "Ten seconds? Why didn't you say so? My wire showing? Is my suit straight? Hair all right? . . . " The cameraman counted down and pointed at the anchorman as the camera light came on.

The anchorman, suddenly cool and collected, looked straight into the camera. "Hello," he said. "This is Dan Splatter with the Six O'clock Ooze News. Today's big story . . . "

With a huge bang and a puff of smoke, Beetlejuice popped onto the news desk. "Stop the presses," he shouted into the camera.

"Huh?" asked a confused Splatter.

"Tonight's top story," said Beetlejuice, leaning

toward the camera, "is . . . Beetlejuice for President!" He fell backwards onto a seat next to Splatter's. "Go ahead, Dan," he said. "Ask me anything."

Splatter looked around to see if anyone would help him out. The camera operator just stared at Beetlejuice, so he decided to wing it. "Uh . . . Okaaay," he said uncertainly. "We have with us in the studio today the ghost . . ."

"With the most!" interrupted Beetlejuice.

" . . . who's . . ."

Beetlejuice turned his hands into a bowl and a spoon and started stirring.

"Causing a stir in the Neitherworld?" Dan asked.

"You bet I am, Dan," said Beetlejuice, spraying batter on Splatter.

"Well, put a lid on it," Splatter hissed. He smirked back at the camera. "So, Beetlejuice. Fill us in on this late-breaking story."

Beetlejuice spread his arms apart. "Spirits," he said easily, "isn't it time the Neitherworld had a president? Someone to lead us down the wrong path—to total irresponsibility! Wildness! Absurdity! Aren't you tired of the same old thing night after night after night? The Neitherworld is too flat, too dull, too boring. Let Beetlejuice put some fizz into your afterlife!"

"But Beetlejuice," said Splatter, "you seem to be

the only ghoul who enjoys your kind of fun. You have fun at the expense of others."

Beetlejuice became a huge, striped head of cabbage. "I've turned over a new leaf!" he cried. He became a stack of coins. "I've changed," he added. "I want to fix things up. I want to make the Neitherworld a better place to live in . . . er . . . that is, a better place to call home."

"Well," said Splatter, pushing Beetlejuice off the desk. "Having a president would be a good thing. I think most ghouls would agree. But is this a one-party race? Who is your opponent?"

"One party race? No sir. Not on my platform!" answered Beetlejuice. Then, looking right into the camera he said, "On the Beetlejuice platform, you'll get as many parties as you want!"

SKREEAWK!!!
The television screen filled with static.

Beetlejuice jumped up from the sofa where he and Lydia were watching the interview back at the Roadhouse. "What's happening?" Beetlejuice demanded.

"We're sorry," came a voice from the television. "We're experiencing operating difficulty."

"No!" cried Beetlejuice. "Not now!" He turned to Lydia. "You gotta understand," he said, turning flat and triangular. "I'm my own best fan."

28

"But how did you answer Dan Splatter?" asked Lydia. "Who will be your opponent?"

"Well Lyds," said Beetlejuice. "Someone running against me would hardly be fair."

"It sure would be," said Lydia. "It's the way all presidents are elected."

"All presidents?"

"All good presidents," said Lydia.

"Well then," said Beetlejuice, stroking his chin. "No problem. I can sense my popularity. Parties every night. Halloween every day!"

"That's the spirit!" said Lydia.

"Where?" Beetlejuice whirled his head around.

"No, no," Lydia corrected herself. "I mean, way to go!"

SKREEK! went the television as the picture returned. The news was over, and a commercial filled the screen.

"Remember, ghouls," went the announcer. "Don't miss today's big political rally down at the Shocking Mall. Meet the next . . . the first . . . president of the Neitherworld! And remember, you too can live in the Neitherworld with dignity!"

"Huh?" Beetlejuice shouted. "How can they have a political rally without the politician? Let's go, Lyds." He transformed himself into a giant wire whisk and, catching Lydia by the arm, propelled her forward. "We've got to whisk right over to the Shocking Mall."

Ghouls and skeletons were gathered around a stage in the center of the Shocking Mall. A banner which read "THE EASY CHOICE FOR PRESIDENT" hung above the stage.

"Wow!" Beetlejuice declared, delighted. "Lyds, I've got to admit this is better than I expected."

"Uh, Beetlejuice," Lydia warned, "something feels wrong about this."

"Did you think I would be so popular, Lyds?" asked Beetlejuice. "I'd better get up there!"

Beetlejuice started winding through the crowd and came to a ghost who was holding his head up in the air, trying to get a better view. "Excuse me," he said, tapping the ghost's shoulder.

The ghost spun his head on his finger as if he was spinning a basketball. When the head stopped, it was facing Beetlejuice, a big cigar clamped firmly between its teeth. "Skip it, Buddy," it said. "I've let enough of you ghouls in front of me!"

"He doesn't get it," Beetlejuice told Lydia. "Boy will he feel stupid when he sees me up on the stage."

"Beetlejuice," Lydia cautioned. "I'm not sure everyone's waiting for you."

"They're not starting to leave?!" Beetlejuice said, sounding alarmed.

A musical voice called out. "Ladies and gentlemen, and other kinds of creatures. Please welcome the easy choice for president."

"Yes! Me!" cried Beetlejuice, jumping for joy.

"A man you all know and love," the voice continued warmly.

"Well, they've got a funny way of showing it," Beetlejuice muttered to Lydia.

An approving murmur rose from the crowd.

"A good ghost. A caring ghost," the voice purred.

"I've got to get up front," Beetlejuice declared.

"Beetlejuice, wait," Lydia cried.

Beetlejuice ignored her. He leaped into the air and started running over the crowd of ghouls, ghosts, goblins, monsters, spiders and skeletons. "Excuse me, pardon me," he begged as he stepped on heads and shoulders. "Sorry, excuse me."

"Ladies and gentlemen and whatever else is out there," repeated the voice. "Please welcome . . ."

"Wait!" cried Beetlejuice.

"Easy Slider!" the voice trilled.

Beetlejuice stopped suddenly, one foot on a big, hairy ball of fur with legs, the other on a scaly creature with tentacles for arms. "What?" he shouted. "Who?"

"Easy Slider," the voice repeated.

"No!" Beetlejuice cried. He stomped up and down.

"Ow," grumbled the ball of fur.

"Listen," Beetlejuice shouted. "I thought up this whole president thing. I'm going to be president. It's only fair."

"You don't have a ghost of a chance!" a loud voice called out in response.

"I do!" Beetlejuice yelled. "Listen, everyone. Forget this Easy Slider guy. He's nothing but a slimeball."

A new voice oozed out of the loudspeakers. "Of course I am. But what a slimeball!"

Beetlejuice stopped raving and looked at the stage.

Something grabbed the microphone. "Hello, Monsters and Mutants," he said in a melodious voice. "I'm Easy Slider. Tell me, do you like my hair-goo?"

The crowd roared its approval.

Easy laughed modestly. "Yes, yes. It's all the work of my personal oozologist. Doesn't he do a wonderful job?"

The crowd cheered, and with good reason. Easy Slider was no ordinary slimeball. His hair-goo was a perfect dark wave across the top of his head. His face had none of the drippiness of ordinary slimeballs, but instead was shaped into

rugged, handsome human features. He had broad cheekbones, a jutting jaw. He wore a flashy suit, with the belt pulled tight, squeezing his body slime up into a broad, impressive chest.

"So," gushed Easy. He grasped his lapels and assumed a solemn expression. "We're here to talk about dignity."

The crowd went wild.

Beetlejuice stomped on the ball of fur and the scaly creature still under his feet. "Stop," he shouted. "This ghoul is a fraud, a slippery con artist. The presidency was my idea."

"So it was," Easy sang. "And I bet you never imagined there would be a candidate better than you running for it."

"No. Only me." Beetlejuice thought for a moment.

"But that's the beauty of a political system," said Easy. "That a bug-infested ghoul like yourself . . . "

"Stop flattering me," Beetlejuice muttered.

" . . . can come up with an idea," Easy continued, gesturing smoothly. "And a dream of a ghost like myself can step in to do the job right."

The ghoulish gathering broke into applause. Beetlejuice tried to speak again, but he was drowned out by the clattering of bones and ghostly howls. Beetlejuice moved back to where Lydia was waiting.

"Lydia," he moaned. "They're ignoring me."

"Don't be scared off by that drip," Lydia said. "You're twice the candidate! Challenge him!"

"Now there's an idea, Lyds!" Beetlejuice said, then took a deep breath, popped his thumb into his mouth, and blew. His body started expanding, rounding out like a balloon. He got bigger and bigger until he floated off the ground.

"Don't let Slider slime you!" Beetlejuice cried. "Listen to Beetlejuice, the ghost with the most! Parties every night, Halloween every day! Whatever you want you'll get!" He had now floated over Easy Slider, casting him in shadow. "I'll be the next president, Slider! Me!"

"Would you care to bet on that?" asked Easy.

"Sure," bellowed Beetlejuice. "If I win, you have to grease my car Doomy for a month."

"And if I win?" asked Easy.

Beetlejuice thought for a moment. "If you win," he declared, "I'll give you the Roadhouse and leave the Neitherworld forever."

Easy smiled. "Beetlejuice, my friend," he said cheerfully. "I accept."

CHAPTER FOUR

EASY SLIDES AHEAD

"EASY SLIDER IS EVERYWHERE!" Beetlejuice screamed.

He and Lydia were in the Roadhouse. They had turned on the television, hoping to catch a mention of Beetlejuice's campaign. Everywhere they looked, though, they saw Easy Slider.

On Channel One, Easy was kissing baby monsters. A long line of waiting mothers stood with their babies. Easy planted a kiss on each baby's forehead—or horns or beak or snout—then handed the tyke back to its mother. An attendant stood next to Easy, wiping off any stray goo his lips might have left behind.

Channel Two showed Easy greeting the local truck-driver's convention. As each truck driver approached him, Easy held out a strong, perfect-looking hand. The truck driver grabbed and squeezed, gooshing Easy Slider's fingers. At the end of the handshake, Easy stuck the deformed mass of goo behind him. His oozologist stamped the goo in a hand mold, shaping another perfect hand for the next truck driver.

Openup Skinfree, the skeleton talk-show host, sat chatting with Easy on Channel Three. Every time Easy spoke, the audience cheered.

"Sleazed to meet you," Easy told a member of the audience. "And always remember this: no matter who I am, I'm not Beetlejuice!"

Openup clapped her bones and shouted, "Yeah! We're having a whopping good slime here!"

Beetlejuice snapped off the television. "Easy Slider is the most popular slimeball in the Neitherworld," he said. "How can I possibly beat him?" He paced the room, head held down.

"I know!" said Lydia, jumping up. "We need to stir up your campaign. And who better to learn from than Delia? She's planning a master campaign for my father right now."

Lydia said Beetlejuice's name three times, and the two of them popped into her room in Peaceful Pines. They immediately dashed down the stairs and peeked into the living room. Delia was sitting on the floor making campaign buttons, a worried Charles on one side of her.

"Stay out of sight," Lydia reminded Beetlejuice.

Delia was talking to Charles. "Remember," she said. "This dinner is very important. You're going to have Nadine Hemlock in the same room with you and Winthrop Adams, your main opponent."

"Dear," said Charles, "why don't we let him run unopposed?"

"Nadine is a very important person," Delia went on. "She's the president of the Sugar Maple Society. Very influential. If you convince her that you're a better candidate than Winthrop Adams, you'll easily win the election."

"Dear?" said Charles.

Delia stamped out a final button. "Now we need bumperstickers."

"Here's a bumpersticker," said Beetlejuice. He flattened his hand into a rectangular sign that said "DELIA FOR TOWN COUNCIL," peeled the paper off the sticky side and slapped it onto Lydia's back.

"Yeow!" cried Lydia, as she flew into the living room. She was still attached to Beetlejuice. He held onto the door and let his body stretch with hers. She flew past her parents. "Hi, Dad," Lydia managed as she whizzed by.

Delia, thumbing through bumper stickers, didn't notice anything.

Lydia reached the end of Beetlejuice's stretching ability, and she shot back into him. As she

38

whipped past Charles, he said absentmindedly, "Hi, Lydia."

Lydia smacked full force into Beetlejuice, and they tumbled out into the hall.

"Beetlejuice," Lydia fumed, "you've got to be more careful around my parents."

"Sorry, babes," said Beetlejuice, smiling. "We needed some exercise."

"Now, Charles," Delia said. "Listen to me."

"Dear?" Charles replied wearily.

"You shouldn't say anything bad. Nobody likes a smear campaign."

Beetlejuice smeared his face on the wall. It was so spread out, Lydia didn't know where to look.

Delia continued. "You just need to make sure nobody mentions Adams."

"Yes, dear," said Charles.

"You want your name on everybody's lips," concluded Delia.

Lydia looked at Beetlejuice's mouth, and saw the word "Charles" printed on his lips.

"Now, Charles," said Delia. "I hope you're as excited about this campaign as I am."

"Overwhelmed, dear," said Charles.

"What a good sport!" said Delia. "Let's pass out these buttons and stickers all over town." She looked around. "Where's Lydia when we need her?"

"Uh-oh," said Lydia. "Let's beat it. Beetlejuice, Beetlejuice, Beetlejuice!"

The thunder that followed startled Delia. "Charles," she gasped. "Did you hear that?"

"What?" said Charles.

Back in the Neitherworld, Beetlejuice and Lydia started walking toward the center of town. As they approached the Shocking Mall, they came across a big, brown pile of muck in the road.

"Yuck!" said Lydia.

"No, Muck," the pile corrected her.

"Yikes!" Beetlejuice jumped back. "Sorry, pal," he added. "I almost stepped on you."

"Happens all the time," answered the Muck, oozing up a little taller. Beetlejuice noticed now that it had eyes and a mouth.

"Well," Beetlejuice nudged Lydia. "Hey, buddy. Pleased to meet you. I'm Beetlejuice."

"I know," slurped the Muck. "You're pretty famous around here."

"You bet I am!" said Beetlejuice. "And I'm here to give you an opportunity to improve the Neitherworld." He produced a button from behind what he thought was the ear of the Muck. It said "BEETLEJUICE FOR PRESIDENT".

"Wait," said Beetlejuice suspiciously. "I know, you're voting for Easy Slider. You're both slime-balls and slimeballs stick together." He paused

and added, "You guys kind of stick to everything."

"Don't talk about Easy Slider," Lydia reminded Beetlejuice. "Talk about yourself."

"I don't much care for Slider," burbled the Muck.

Beetlejuice grinned. "You don't?" he asked.

"He's a little too stiff for my taste," the Muck continued. "I'm proud to be muck. I'll drip wherever I want. Easy Slider tries too hard to look like a solid citizen."

Beetlejuice looked the Muck over for a moment, then handed the button to Lydia. "Can you pin this on him?" he asked.

Lydia sank the pin into the brown ooze.

"Muck, my friend," Beetlejuice declared, "if I'm elected, I plan to institute a laziness policy. Ghouls move around too much. I plan to make everyone gain at least ten pounds and generally get looser." Beetlejuice started sagging. His feet melted and turned into puddles.

"That would be nice," the Muck answered.

"Nice!" Beetlejuice cried. "Why, it'll be more than just nice. It'll be revolutionary. Just think of the benefits of turning everyone into slimeballs. We won't need park benches. We won't need seatbelts. No more broken bones."

They left the Muck and continued on their way. Beetlejuice was feeling better about himself. They found Easy Slider standing on the stage at the Shocking Mall, talking to a crowd of onlookers. "Folks," Easy shouted into his microphone. "Isn't it true that you spent your lives trying to impress people? Always rushing about? Now you should be able to impress your fellow ghouls without ever trying to! My fellow Neitherworldlians, I say to you: Give me dignity or give me another afterlife!"

Beetlejuice grabbed a cup of Coka-Goola from an audience member. Pouring the drink out on the ground, he mixed the goo in the dirt. "What's a campaign without a little mud slinging," he chuckled, grabbing some of the oozy brown stuff.

"Open wide, Slider," called Beetlejuice, and he slung the mud.

"Well, folks, I say 'Read my drips' . . . ". Easy's mouth was wide open when the mud hit him. He coughed and sputtered, spitting out globs of mud. "Who's responsible for this?" he demanded.

"What's the matter?" Beetlejuice shouted. "Not up to a little unhealthy competition?"

"You don't know what competition is," snarled Easy. He addressed the crowd: "Let it be known that I challenge Beetlejuice to a public debate on the presidency of the Neitherworld."

"Ha!" cried Beetlejuice. "And let it be known that I accept the challenge!"

CHAPTER FIVE

A HEATED DEBATE

"LADIES, GENTLEMEN, and things that go bump in the night, this is Dan Splatter bringing you live coverage of the Neitherworld Presidential Debate. This promises to be an exciting battle. The incredibly smooth Easy Slider, a candidate whose personality really sticks to you, will debate head to head, drip to prank, with Beetlejuice, a ghoul who needs no introduction. Indeed, some people feel he needs to be told when to leave.

"The panel of experts who will question our two candidates today include Jacques La Lean, fitness freak of the Neitherworld.

"Joining Jacques is the Monster from Across the Street. We don't know if he has anything to ask, but he wanted to be on the show and when he wants something, we give it to him." Splatter tried to keep his distance from the Monster.

"Also on our panel of experts is Poopsie, the Monster's dog. Heh-heh. Ah! here come our candidates now."

Beetlejuice made a grand entrance. He did his special merry-go-round scare trick. A ring of dancing goblins spun around his head while his arms, like long hoses, whipped out over the entire audience. He showered everyone with a confetti of dried worms and squid bits. The crowd ate it up. Literally. Then Beetlejuice turned himself into a ferris wheel and rolled over to his podium. Lydia stood in the wings watching him.

Easy Slider quietly crossed the stage. His hair-goo was perfectly shaped. He was wearing a super fancy suit and dark sunglasses. Smiling broadly, he put his hands to his lips and blew kisses to the audience. The hot lights made his hands stick to his lips, and strings of slime stretched between them as he spread his arms wide. His personal oozologist rushed onto the stage to tidy him up.

Dan Splatter stepped up to the center microphone, between the two podiums. "All right, fright fans," he said. "We all know why we're here. Let's have the first question."

Jacques stood up. "Byetelzhooze," he said, "how would you improve ze Neitherworld?"

Beetlejuice jabbed his finger in the air. "I'm glad you asked that," he said. "Look around you." He gestured widely. "What do you see? The same old unspeakable horrors, day after day. Ghosts and goblins. Mutations and monsters. Now think of how your afterlife could be improved. Imagine beaches lapped with shark-infested waters. Tires washed up on the shores. Oil slicks on the water."

The crowd murmured its approval.

Beetlejuice leaned forward. "Let's make the Neitherworld the land of a thousand points of fright!"

The crowd roared.

Easy Slider butted in. "I agree absolutely. But I've taken things a step farther. I've already contracted with chemical plants and nuclear reactors to provide us with all the toxic and radioactive waste we could ever want. Free delivery."

Howls of glee filled the Mall.

"He's trying to steal my thunder," Beetlejuice said to himself. "I can't let that happen." He cracked some lightning and thunder between his fingers, then said into his microphone, "I congratulate Easy Slider on his effort, but as usual he falls short." Beetlejuice crumpled to half his normal size and tumbled onto the stage. He popped back to normal. "He wants to have the nuclear plants deliver waste to the beach. I plan to have the plants themselves on the beach. Imagine sunning yourself right next to a nuclear reactor. What a tan you'd get!"

Bones clattered everywhere. Easy muttered to himself and cast Beetlejuice an angry look.

The Monster from Across the Street stood up. "There's been some talk," he bellowed, "about a lot of French poodles. What do you have to say about that?" Poopsie wagged his tail.

As Easy scratched his head, his finger sank deep into his hair-goo. "I have no idea what you're talking about," he responded.

Beetlejuice cackled madly. "Of course not," he cried, yanking his head off his shoulders. "Easy Slider is disconnected from the Neitherworld's real issues."

"Byetelzhooze," said Jacques. "Tell us about ze exercise program you have in mind for ze Neitherworld."

"Uh-oh," Beetlejuice muttered to himself. He wondered if the Muck he had stumbled across was in the audience, or watching from home. "I think everyone knows where I stand on that," Beetlejuice answered.

"Ah, let me not answer that question!" said Easy.

"Spoken like a true slimeball," said Beetlejuice, as he dripped into a puddle and re-formed. "My opponent has no backbone. Won't take a stand.

Can't take a stand with slime for feet." He started dancing. "My program ensures that you exercise every part of your body." His body broke into pieces, which started dancing with one another.

"But Byetlezhooze," cried Jacques. "I've never seen you exercise before."

"I think we've had enough on this topic," said Beetlejuice. He collected his body parts. "It's no good beating a dead horse."

A horse in the audience neighed loudly.

"Yeah," Beetlejuice added under his breath. "Those dead horses can be nasty."

"Byetelzhooze," said Jacques. "It takes a lot of work to be ze president. Have you ever done a stitch of work in your afterlife?"

Easy Slider chuckled.

Beetlejuice wiped the sweat off his brow. "Work," he cried. He peeled the skin off his hand. "Why, I've worked my fingers to the bone." He dropped his head down between his knees, emitting a loud cracking noise. "I've broken my back. I've driven myself till I was an empty shell of a man." He pulled open his coat to reveal the empty space inside it.

"I'm on a roll now," he told himself. He turned into a ball and bounced to center stage.

"Did you know," he announced to the crowd as

he became his usual ugly self, "in my previous life I had forty-seven different jobs, each one harder than the one before it. So when I got here, I figured I'd give myself a break. Now it's time to work again. I'm ready for it."

The audience cheered wildly.

Beetlejuice ran to the side of the stage where Lydia was standing. "How am I doing?" he asked.

"Great!" said Lydia enthusiastically. "Beetlejuice, I didn't know you used to have forty-seven jobs."

"Are you joking, babes?" Beetlejuice chuckled. "I never did a stitch of work." He bounded back onstage.

Easy Slider raised his arms for attention. His hair-goo was beginning to melt under the hot lights. His oozologist ran out and tried to re-shape it, but the hair-goo was too loose. "Ahem," said Easy into his microphone. "I, too, worked hard in my previous life. Beetlejuice claims he had forty-seven jobs. Well, I had fifty-seven!"

Beetlejuice laughed. "There you go again!" he said. "Whatever I say, you try to improve on." He turned to the audience. "Does Easy Slider ever come up with his own ideas? No! He tries to say whatever you want to hear, to be whatever you want him to be, but he isn't really anything at all!"

Easy sputtered with rage. His skin turned

green, and his hair-goo dripped into his eyes. "That's not true!" he said.

"Sure," said Beetlejuice. "This drip has mistaken dullness for dignity. Do you really want to spend your time being dignified? Who do you need to impress?"

"Don't believe him," said Easy. His voice sounded bubbly and gurgly.

"Oh, sure," said Beetlejuice. "You're dripping with sincerity!"

Easy wiped his hair-goo aside. "I'm dripping because of these hot lights," he complained.

"You're just a sore loser," said Beetlejuice. He floated into the air and reclined comfortably. "Come on," he pleaded. "Admit it. You need me to be President of the Neitherworld. Who would want a slimy character like Easy Slider?"

"This isn't fair," sputtered Easy. His speech came out garbled since his lips were melting together. "These hot lights are unfair to a slime-ball."

"Is it the lights?" Beetlejuice asked, turning himself into a frying pan. "Or is it the grilling you're getting?"

Easy swatted at Beetlejuice. A gob of goo came loose from his arm and splatted against his opponent.

"I've got to hand it to you," laughed Beetlejuice, wiping off the ooze and tossing it back.

The crowd laughed with him.

"I'll get even with you," snarled Easy Slider. "This race isn't over yet." He turned to the audience, but as he did so, his legs oozed together. Easy was melting into the stage. "Listen, ghouls," he cried. "Forget about this debate. It's not fair to Slimeballs. It's not dignified!" But his voice faded as he sank away from the microphone. His oozologist rushed onto the stage and put his arm around Easy's shoulders. He mopped Easy off the stage, then rushed back with a sponge and sopped up all the stray slime Easy had left behind.

"Ha-ha!" cried Beetlejuice, inflating himself to four times his normal size. "Thank you everyone, thank you." He shot off fireworks from his hands. He produced confetti and balloons that read "HALLOWEEN EVERY DAY." Here and there he zapped bumper stickers onto people's foreheads. "Beetlejuice for President!"

Lydia was thrilled. Beetlejuice was doing great. It really looked like he might win. Now if only she could get him to think seriously about being a real president!

CHAPTER SIX

BEETLEJUICE JOINS THE CLUB

"I DON'T SEE WHY we need to be here," Beetlejuice complained.

He and Lydia were back in Peaceful Pines. Lydia had dragged Beetlejuice to the Peaceful Pines Country Club, where Charles and Delia were attending a candidates' party. "I just thought we could pick up some more campaign tips by watching my parents in action," said Lydia.

"What do I need with campaign tips?" asked Beetlejuice. "I'm winning. I'm the chief tomato." He became round and red. "I stomped on my competition. He'll never ketchup."

"You never know," said Lydia. "The race isn't over until it's over."

"Till the fat lady sings, huh?" said Beetlejuice.

He started to transform his body, but then thought better of it.

"We should always be prepared for last-minute surprises," said Lydia. Under her breath, she added, "Especially with the campaign you've been running."

Beetlejuice pointed toward the country club building. "I can't go in and just mingle," he said.

"I'll go mingle," said Lydia. "You hang around somewhere and watch."

With a puff of smoke Beetlejuice turned himself into a bat. "Good idea," he said, and flew off.

When Lydia went through the front door, Beetlejuice flew down the chimney. They both reached the lounge, where the party was in progress, at the same moment.

Delia and Charles were standing in a small crowd of people. Delia had her hand on Charles's back. "I bet she'd rather have a leash," Beetlejuice said, making himself into a collar to slip around Charles's neck.

A much larger crowd was gathered around a handsome, self-assured looking man in a leisure suit. Lydia guessed he was Winthrop Adams.

Lydia walked over to her parents' crowd. Beetlejuice turned himself into a spider and crawled across the ceiling.

A woman in the crowd said, "Mr. Deetz, the developers promise lots of new jobs for the townspeople. Don't you want that?"

"Yes, well," said Charles. He thought for a moment. Finally he said, "Um."

Delia stepped forward. "Just think what it would do to the town if they put up a factory in the woods. Acres of land would be spoiled. Think of all the noise and pollution."

"That's true," said the woman.

"Way to go, mom," said Lydia.

"Yes, dear," said Charles. "Exactly."

Up on the ceiling, Beetlejuice turned himself into a miniature, upside-down factory. "I like noise and pollution," he said, and he started spewing smoke.

A man stepped forward. "But the developers promised to build a new park, not a factory."

"Well," said Charles. "Yes."

Delia raised her finger. "What's a park compared to the natural beauty of the forest? The developers are trying to bribe the town!"

"Precisely," said Charles.

"It's clear who's running this campaign," cried Beetlejuice, turning back into himself. He walked upside-down along the ceiling. "Let's see how the other guy is doing."

Lydia noticed Beetlejuice moving and followed him. She walked into the crowd surrounding Winthrop Adams.

"You," said Winthrop, pointing to a man in the crowd. "You own the town market. Just think how much business you would do with the park . . . er, factory. All those workers buying lunches."

"And you," he said to another. "You run the town snowplow. Imagine how much more work you'll have when they put a new highway right through town."

"What?" cried Lydia.

"That's terrible," Lydia said to Winthrop. "You're asking everyone to give up this beautiful town just to make a little more money."

"My dear girl," Winthrop said. "You're just a child. How can you hope to understand the way the world works?"

"I know enough to know that you're a phoney," said Lydia. "You're just trying to do anything the developers want. You don't care at all about our town."

Winthrop laughed at her. "Run along, now. We're trying to have a serious discussion."

Lydia angrily stomped off. Beetlejuice followed her out of the room. They found themselves in the restaurant. "I told you it was a waste," Beetlejuice said. "This is the most boring group of people I've ever seen. They belong in the Neitherworld."

"Beetlejuice," said Lydia. "Don't you see how important this election is? If Winthrop Adams wins, developers will ruin the town."

Beetlejuice shook his head. "I'd start looking for a new town, then, because old Charles doesn't have much of a chance."

"There's still Nadine Hemlock," Lydia said. "If Charles manages to impress her, she could get the entire Sugar Maple Society to vote for him."

"It'll never happen," said Beetlejuice. "He's too dull and he's too honest."

"Too honest?" Lydia asked.

"He needs to stretch the truth a bit," Beetlejuice said, stretching his arms ten feet apart. "He needs to impress people. Like that Winthrop guy. He's telling people exactly what they want to hear."

Suddenly Beetlejuice had an idea. "Come with me," he said. "I'll show you what it takes to get elected. All you've got to do," Beetlejuice declared, "is tell people exactly what they want to hear. Just lie a little, and people love you for it."

"It's not that easy," Lydia said.

"Sure it is," Beetlejuice assured her. He turned into a giant pitcher. "You just have to pour on the charm. Watch this."

Assuming his normal form, Beetlejuice approached a nearby table where some appetizers had been set out for the guests. A nervous-looking man wearing a large chef's hat paced up and down behind it.

"Why look here, Lydia," said Beetlejuice, "this gentleman has been kind enough to provide some refreshments for us." He popped a cracker spread with chopped liver and garlic into his mouth.

"Why, this is delicious," he said to the chef, trying not to gag. "And so is this," he continued as he ate a concoction of hot peppers and marsh-mallows. "Did you make these scrumptious tid-bits yourself?"

"Ah, you are too kind, my dear sir," the chef said, beaming. "These appetizers are made from my own recipes. Each is absolutely unique."

"No, " Beetlejuice gasped. "Well, I must say, I've never tasted anything like them. Say, babes. I'm running for town council. Name's Charles Deetz. Vote for me, babes."

Beetlejuice returned to Lydia. "See, Lyds," he said. "I've learned something about campaigning. You've got to go out and meet the people. They've got to like you if you want them to vote for you. Easy Slider just looks down on people. But me, I'm a regular ghoul at the pool, a spirit who can hear it."

"That's all true," said Lydia. "But people expect you to live up to your promises."

"Who cares?" Beetlejuice laughed. "By then I'll already be president. I'll be able to do whatever I want."

"That's not how it works," Lydia said.

The two of them wandered outside onto the golf course. At the first hole they met a golfer. He was a scrawny guy with inch-thick glasses. Even with the glasses, he couldn't see a thing. As Beetlejuice and Lydia watched, the fellow carefully lined up his feet, drew back his club, and swung with all his might.

Swish!

"Did I hit it?" the man asked them.

"Missed it by a mile," Beetlejuice muttered.

"Oh well," said the man. "Can you tell me if I am facing in the right direction?" He was facing the clubhouse.

"Right direction for what?" asked Beetlejuice.

The man scratched his head. "I am on the golf course, aren't I?"

"Here," said Lydia, stepping forward. "Let me help you." She took the man by the shoulders and turned him till he was facing the fairway. "Try that," she said.

"Thank you," the man said warmly. He planted

his feet wide apart. He shook his hips, took a few practice swings, and then swung his club back. The force of his swing pulled him around so he was facing the clubhouse again. Down came the golf club and—*Whack*—the ball went flying.

It crashed through a clubhouse window.

"Well I'll be!" cried Beetlejuice. "A hole in one!"

"Really?" asked the bewildered man.

"I've never seen anything like it," continued Beetlejuice, grabbing the man by the arm and leading him across the lawn. "What a graceful arc! Two gentle bounces on the green and it rolled straight into the hole."

"Oh my!" said the man.

"My friend," said Beetlejuice. "You're a pro. Hit the golf circuit. You're a sensation."

As they reached the hole, Beetlejuice pulled a ball from thin air and tossed it into the hole. The man got down on his knees and fumbled around till he found the hole. He reached inside and, sure enough, there was a ball in it. "Hey," he cried. "I really did get a hole in one!"

"You bet," Beetlejuice said. "By the way, my name's Charles Deetz. I'm running for town council. I think there might be a place for you on our recreation board."

"My goodness," gasped the man. "I hope you win."

Beetlejuice chuckled. "It's in your hands now," he said.

Beetlejuice and Lydia left the man swinging away at hole two. "See," Beetlejuice said, "I'll promise anything to get votes."

"Beetlejuice," Lydia said, "it's going to get you into trouble. That man never got a hole-in-one. Sooner or later he'll figure out you were lying to him, and then he'll be really mad at you. Or mad at my father."

"Fiddlesticks," Beetlejuice declared. "Lies work wonders."

"They do not," Lydia said.

"Do so," said Beetlejuice. "I'll show you how much I believe in them. I hereby cast a spell on myself: From now on, every word I say in the campaign will be a lie."

"That sounds like trouble," said Lydia. She looked at her watch. "Uh-oh, it's almost time for Delia's dinner party for Charles. Nadine Hemlock's going to be here for it. Sorry, Beetlejuice," she said. "I've got to go inside."

Beetlejuice rubbed his hands together. "Oh boy," he said. "A dinner party. This is something I definitely don't want to miss."

CHAPTER SEVEN

MY PIG IS COOKED

DELIA HAD RENTED out the country club dining room, but she was doing all the cooking herself. Lydia was greeting people at the door.

"Boy, I got back just in time," Lydia said. She opened the front door for the town mayor, a meek man with a trim mustache.

Before Lydia could close the door and welcome the mayor, a huge, black limousine drove up. The driver jumped out, dashed around to the passenger's door, and quickly opened it. Out walked a tall, thin woman dressed in a severe red suit. Her lipstick matched the color of her outfit exactly.

"Be a good girl," said the woman, striding past Lydia, "and tell your mother Nadine Hemlock is here."

Lydia scurried after Nadine, into the dining room where the other guests were gathered.

Nadine stopped in the doorway. She surveyed the room and she frowned.

Someone was saying, "I was hoping, Mr. Mayor, that you could start a health-awareness program. Nothing big, just posters in the schools and things like that. Perhaps Mr. Deetz could help push it through the town council."

Nadine's icy voice rang out. "Nothing is more important than the environment. The Sugar Maple Society is concerned with nothing else."

All conversation stopped. Just then Delia entered the room with a tray full of glasses and broke the ice.

"Ah," she chirped, "Nadine! Now we can begin. Let's start with some apple cider. Homemade, of course." She passed the drinks around. "Lydia," she whispered. "Go find your father, dear."

Lydia found Charles in the club room, reading the newspaper. "Dad," she said. "It's dinner time."

Charles lowered the paper and regarded his daughter. "No dear, we're having guests for dinner. The mayor. And Nadine Hemlock. I'm to impress them."

"They're here, Dad," said Lydia, impatiently.

"Well, why didn't you say so?" Charles asked.

He got up and hurried into the dining room. Lydia followed close behind.

Nadine Hemlock was shouting at the mayor. "We can no longer be passive about this. We need a strong leader on the town council. A dynamic leader. I don't care what he stands for. I'll tell him what to stand for."

"Boy," Lydia said under her breath. "This woman would like Beetlejuice's style just fine."

Beetlejuice, meanwhile, was haunting a corner of the ceiling. "This Nadine Hemlock is a real spitfire," he said to himself. His head burst into flames. "I've got to spice up this party a bit." And with a flash, he disappeared.

"Tra-la," sang Delia, waltzing into the room with a tray of bowls. "For an appetizer, apple soup!"

Nadine arched her eyebrow. "Are we on an apple theme, then?"

"Ha-ha," tittered Delia. "Natural, you know. We grew them ourselves. Isn't that right, dear?" she asked her husband.

But Charles was busy slurping away at his soup. "Huh?" he said. "What's next?"

"A-ha-ha," sang Delia. "The main course. It's time for the main course." She dashed out of the room. In a minute she was back with more bowls. "Applesauce," she said. "But don't worry. It's just a side dish." She dashed away again and in a moment returned with a new tray. On the tray was an entire roast suckling pig. Of course, there was an apple in its mouth. "Ta- da," cried Delia.

"Oh," said Nadine. "How simply horrid! I hate pigs so."

"Well you're not going to talk to it," Lydia muttered under her breath. "You're just going to eat it."

"What's that, dear?" asked Nadine icily.

"Nothing," Lydia said.

Suddenly something weird happened. The applesauce in all the bowls started bubbling.

Charles started slapping at his sauce with a spoon, trying to calm it down.

"Uh-oh," Lydia said to herself. "I've got a feeling I know what's happening."

The bowls started shaking and rattling. Suddenly the bowl in front of Nadine let out a loud pop. Applesauce splattered onto her dress. "Oh," cried Nadine. "How awful. My new dress."

With a violent snort, the suckling pig spit the apple out of its mouth and leapt to its feet.

"Go Beetlejuice!" Lydia whispered.

Hooves scrabbling on the tabletop, the pig started running around the table. It grunted and squealed as it ran, shaking its head up and down.

"Why," cried Delia. "I cooked that pig! It can't be running."

"Apparently you didn't cook it enough," some-one shouted from under the table.

"Of all the . . ." cried Nadine, terrified. "Keep it away from me!"

The pig suddenly stopped running and, spreading its front hooves, started tap dancing. It was still snorting and squealing, but the squeals sounded vaguely like "Charles, Charles, Charles."

"What's happening?" cried Nadine.

"This can't be," cried Delia. "My party's ruined." Without thinking, Delia jumped up on her chair and dove at the pig. She caught it around the belly, and the two of them tumbled off the table and onto the floor. "Take that!" cried Delia, tugging at one hoof. "And that!"

"Dad!" Lydia cried. "Do something."

But Charles had noticed that his applesauce had stopped shaking and he was busy eating again, doing his best to ignore the noise around him.

The grunting and snorting continued for a few seconds. Then with a long squeal, the pig squirmed out of Delia's arms. Before anyone could catch it, it gave a terrific jump and sailed out the window. The sound of its hooves clattering on the driveway gradually faded into the distance.

A long minute passed.

"Oh dear," Delia said finally. "There goes our dinner."

Nadine bounded over and snatched Delia off the ground. "My dear," she said. "I've never seen such bravery in my life."

"Oh, really?" Delia said, looking dazed.

"All this campaigning is hogwash," Nadine said. "I'll take you out for dinner, and we can discuss the Sugar Maple Society's endorsement of your husband's campaign, just between us."

"Oh," said Delia, clapping her hands together. "I'd be delighted. Charles, come along."

"Really, Delia," said Nadine. "We don't need him. And with Delia in her clutches, Nadine swept out of the room.

Lydia ran outside, where Beetlejuice was waiting for her. "That was great!" Lydia said, slapping him on the back. "That was the funniest thing I've ever seen."

"Funny, maybe, but nobody credits me." Beetlejuice complained.

"Well," said Lydia. "We'd better get out of here for a while. Lay low until everything cools off."

"You know what to do, babes," said Beetlejuice.

"I sure do," Lydia answered. She held up her arms and called out:

"Beetlejuice, Beetlejuice, Beetlejuice!"

CHAPTER EIGHT

BEETLEJUICE'S DREAM

"BEETLEJUICE," said Lydia. "Do you want to hear some of my ideas for your governing strategy?"

"Huh? What?" Beetlejuice murmured. He was lying on a cushion of air, gently floating around his room at the Roadhouse. Lydia was sitting at a table writing notes on a piece of paper. "What are you talking about?" Beetlejuice asked.

"A governing strategy," Lydia stated. "Since things are looking so good for you in the Ooze News poll, I thought you should start planning what you'll do when you win the election."

"Lyds, Babes," Beetlejuice assured her. "I *am* ready. Nobody's ever been more ready than me."

"Beetlejuice, be serious," Lydia said. "You haven't given it any thought."

"You're wrong," said Beetlejuice. "Why, I've got a standing order with the Gross-Out Importing company. As soon as I win the election, they're set to import some of the finest, gooiest, stickiest bugs from all corners of the Neitherworld. I'm going to throw the biggest, most disgusting celebration the Neitherworld has ever seen."

Lydia giggled. "That's fine if you want to have a party. But I'm talking about after the party."

Beetlejuice bounced down to the floor. He spread his arms wide. "My entire presidency will be one big celebration," he said. "Halloween every day." He draped an arm around Lydia's shoulders. "How would you like to come into a dream of my new life?"

"Neat," said Lydia. "I've never been inside someone else's dream before."

"Come with me," Beetlejuice said. He snapped his fingers and a doorway appeared. "After you," he said, ushering Lydia through the door.

Lydia looked all around. "This side of the door looks just like the other side," she complained.

"Of course," agreed Beetlejuice. "I'll still live in the Roadhouse. No need to change my room."

"I don't get it," Lydia said, scratching her head.

"Follow me." Beetlejuice took her hand and led her into the lobby of the Roadhouse.

Jacques La Lean was in the lobby, dressed for

his morning jog. "Ah, President Byetelzhooze," he called. "I am reaady to work out. Care to join me?"

"Nope," Beetlejuice said, picking his teeth.

"But Byetelzhooze, what about your exercise program?"

Beetlejuice tossed his hands in the air. "I don't like to exercise," he said.

Jacques laughed. "Of course. Ha-ha."

"Wait a minute," Lydia said. "Jacques, aren't you mad that there's no exercise program?"

"Of course not," Jacques answered.

"But Beetlejuice promised one," said Lydia.

Jacques shrugged. "Byetelzhooze is ze president. He can do anything he wants." Jacques bounded happily out of the Roadhouse.

Lydia turned to Beetlejuice, annoyed. "It won't be like that," she said.

"Sure it will, babes," said Beetlejuice with a wink. "Trust me."

An unfamiliar ghoul came up to fan Beetlejuice. Another appeared to give him a manicure. "Just rough my nails up a bit," Beetlejuice told him. "Don't knock off any of the mold."

Ginger the spider came into the room. "Beetlejuice," she whined. "I just went to the store to buy some shoes. When I looked in my bag, I saw they had only given me two shoes."

Beetlejuice sucked some stray bug parts from between his teeth. "Of course, babes. Shoes come in pairs."

"You told me they'd come in sets of eight," Ginger said.

"So, but four pairs," Beetlejuice said.

"Okay," said Ginger. "You're the president. Say, want to see my latest dance?"

"Be a doll, Ginger," said Beetlejuice. "Go and dance for the Monster Across the Street."

"Anything you say," Ginger said eagerly. "You're the president." And she dashed out.

"Hey," Beetlejuice said to Lydia. "Make a note. I hereby declare this month to be National Prank Month. I'm going to play a trick on everyone in the Neitherworld before the month is over."

"Beetlejuice," Lydia said. "I'm not your secretary."

"Sorry, Lyds," Beetlejuice's head fell to the floor. "I got ahead of myself for a moment. Shall we step outside?"

"I'm not sure I'm ready for this," Lydia said.

Before they could get outside, there was a knock on the door. Beetlejuice pulled it open. A mail carrier stood outside, holding a huge sack. He handed the sack to Beetlejuice.

"What's this?" Beetlejuice demanded.

"Taxes," said the carrier.

Beetlejuice threw open the sack. It was filled to the brim with money. "Oh, yeah!" said Beetlejuice. "Now it's party time!"

"Beetlejuice, this is ridiculous," Lydia said.

"Quiet, Lyds," said Beetlejuice. "Take some of this." He held out a fistful of dollars.

"Are you trying to bribe me?" asked Lydia.

Beetlejuice shrugged. "Works with everyone else. Now come on, let's go outside."

They stepped out onto the front lawn of the Roadhouse. As they did, a cheer arose from thousands of ghouls that were gathered there. A group of Head-hunters, huge heads on legs with bones through their noses, rushed forward. "Oh great Beetlejuice," cried the head Head. "We have worked long and hard, we have traveled far and wide. We bring you, at great personal expense and suffering, the rarest bug in the world: the three-spotted, iridescent, double-twist grunge beetle."

"Thanks guys," Beetlejuice said. He picked up the bug and tossed it into his mouth. Crunch-smack-crunch-smack-swallow, went his jaws. "Great stuff," he said. "Get me twenty more."

The Head-hunters ran off.

"Come off it, Beetlejuice," claimed Lydia. "You don't really think life will be like this, do you?"

"I'm the president," Beetlejuice said in a bored

tone of voice. "Life will be however I want it to be. Hey, look over there."

Lydia looked where Beetlejuice was pointing. A forty-foot tall statue of him dominated the skyline.

"Beetlejuice," Lydia protested. "You don't seem to understand. A president serves the people. They don't serve you," she cried as she ran back.

"Wait, wait, Lyds," Beetlejuice called desperately, running after her. "Where are you going?"

"I'm leaving this ridiculous dream," Lydia said, storming back into Beetlejuice's room. The door to reality was still open, and she walked in.

Beetlejuice came through behind her and the door disappeared. "Calm down, Lydia," he pleaded. "It was only a dream."

Lydia wheeled around and pointed at him. "Beetlejuice," she said, "you have totally lost sight of why someone runs for president."

"But," Beetlejuice said.

"No 'but's," said Lydia. "Unless you straighten up and fly right, I'm through with this campaign. You've been lying to everyone. To yourself. Maybe you're even lying to me."

"Lydia," cried Beetlejuice, horrified. "You're my best friend. I swear I would never lie to you!"

"Hmph!" said Lydia. With that she stormed out of the Roadhouse. She stalked down the street, fuming mad. "That Beetlejuice," she muttered.

"Why can't he think of anyone but himself? I mean, sure I like him because he's sneaky and devious. But still, when it comes to being president you've got to care about something more than just having a good time."

As she turned a corner, she saw Easy Slider addressing a crowd of ghouls. "What's this?" Lydia wondered. Trying not to attract attention to herself, she crept forward.

"Beetlejuice promises fun for the Neitherworld," Easy cried. "But all he cares about is fun for Beetlejuice. Do you think he means the things he's promised you? Maybe you should ask your friends what Beetlejuice has promised *them.*"

"Uh-oh," Lydia moaned. "I was afraid of this."

Everyone was there: Jacques La Lean, the Muck, Ginger. The ghouls started talking amongst themselves. An angry murmur rose as they realized how many lies Beetlejuice had told them.

Easy drew himself up taller. "Every word out of Beetlejuice's mouth is a lie. He's not capable of speaking one true word."

"That's a pretty strong thing to say," the Monster from Across the Street called out.

"Yes," Jacques agreed.

"True enough," Easy responded. "But I'm willing to back up those words with action. I'm willing to stake my claim on the presidency. I say we put Beetlejuice in a lie detector. If he can answer one question truthfully, I'll resign from the race."

The crowd whooped and hollered.

"But," Easy continued, "if he can't answer a question truthfully, what are we going to do with him?"

"String him up," the Monster shouted.

"Chop off his head," countered the Muck.

"Tar and feather him," someone else suggested.

"He'd enjoy all that," Easy Slider said. "No, I have something much more appropriate in mind."

"What ees eet?" asked Jacques.

Easy gave the crowd a sinister grin. "If Beetlejuice can't answer one question truthfully, we'll banish him to the Land of the Sandworms!" he declared.

A gasp rose from the crowd. Then howls. Then wild applause. People loved the idea. Giant Sandworms were the one thing Beetlejuice feared most in the Neitherworld.

Lydia shrunk back in horror. She remembered the spell Beetlejuice had put on himself at the country club. He had vowed not to speak a word of truth until the election was over.

CHAPTER NINE

YOU MAKE YOUR BED, YOU LIE IN IT

"BEETLEJUICE!" cried Lydia, bursting through the door. "You're in big trouble."

"Hey, calm down, Lyds," said Beetlejuice. "What's the problem?"

"The problem," Lydia said, "is the angry mob coming your way. They want to put you in a lie detector and ask you a bunch of questions."

"So?" Beetlejuice asked. "What's the big deal?"

"The big deal," said Lydia, "is if you don't answer their questions truthfully, they're going to banish you to the Land of the Sandworms."

Beetlejuice's eyes popped out of his head. "Sandworms?" he shrieked. "I hate sandworms. There's nothing worse. They're big. They're ugly. They eat you for breakfast. Then they eat you again for dinner. What am I going to do?"

Lydia picked up his eyeballs and pushed them back into their sockets. "I'd suggest you start telling the truth," she said.

"I'd like to, Lyds," Beetlejuice said. "I really would. But there's a little problem. I put a spell on myself. I can't tell the truth about anything until after the election's over, remember?"

Lydia crossed her arms and glared at Beetlejuice. "Well just break the spell," she said.

"It's not that easy," Beetlejuice moaned. "When I cast a spell, I'm stuck with it.

"I told you all your lies would get you into trouble," said Lydia.

Beetlejuice dashed to the window and peered out. The mob was swarming over the junk in the yard. Spirits were circling the Roadhouse.

"Maybe I can sneak out the back," Beetlejuice cried. He ran to the back door and flung it open. Jacques was there with even more ghouls.

"You can't escape, Byetelzhooze," said Jacques.

"Jacques, pal," Beetlejuice pleaded. "Just look the other way while I skip town, huh?"

"Perhaps eef you ask me in French," Jacques suggested.

"I don't know French," Beetlejuice cried.

"But, Byetelzhooze," Jacques said sarcastically. "I thought everyone in ze Neitherworld would speak French eef you were President."

"Yikes," cried Beetlejuice. He slammed the door shut. "Lydia," he moaned, running back into the lobby. "This doesn't look good. Why don't you just mention my name three times or so and we can pop out of here until this whole thing blows over."

Lydia nodded eagerly. "Beetlejuice," she said.

Beetlejuice sighed with relief.

"Beetlejuice," she said again.

Then she stopped.

"What's the matter, babes?" asked Beetlejuice. "Why are you stopping there?"

"You can't hide from this forever," she said. "Sooner or later you have to face these people."

"Yeah, well, later would be better," Beetlejuice explained. "After the election, when I can tell the truth again. Now, come on. Time's running out."

Lydia frowned and thought for a moment. Her mouth started forming Beetlejuice's name. "Bee—"

Beetlejuice nodded eagerly.

Lydia stopped again. "No," she declared. "I can't do it. I want you to win on your merits."

"Lydia, what are you saying?" Beetlejuice cried.

"I'm saying," Lydia answered, "you make your bed, you lie in it. Er . . . so to speak."

"Lydia," Beetlejuice wailed. "How could you do this to me?"

"I didn't," Lydia answered. "You did it to yourself."

Beetlejuice gave her a long, forlorn look. Then he straightened up. "Okay," he said. "Fine. I've lied just fine so far. I'll just lie to the lie detector. I mean, how well do those things really work anyway?" He poked his chin in the air and strode to the front door. "Here goes," he said bravely.

As he stepped outside, an eerie chant reached his ears. "Liar . . . Liar . . . Liar . . ."

"Hi, frights," Beetlejuice laughed nervously.

"Liar . . . Liar . . ." the crowd continued.

"You've got me all wrong," Beetlejuice explained. "I mean, sure I've made a few mistakes. I've told people some things that weren't exactly true. But those were honest mistakes."

The crowd parted, and Beetlejuice stopped talking.

Easy Slider, pulling a rope, came toward Beetlejuice. The rope was attached to a large wooden platform. Sitting on the platform was a huge flower pot, with a lie detector inside.

It was a fiendish-looking thing. Thick green vines and tendrils rose out of the dirt. At the end of some of the vines were beaklike mouths, with vicious, gnashing teeth. Other vines were simply long and snakelike, and they whipped back and forth furiously. In the center of the whole mess was a pad of red bristles. They hummed and vibrated strangely.

Easy Slider clapped his hands, and before Beetlejuice could say a word the snakelike vines lashed out and snatched him off the ground. They wrapped themselves around him, pinning his arms to his sides.

"Those vines," said Easy Slider, "have a sticky stuff on them that's strong enough to keep you from disappearing."

"Yikes," said Beetlejuice.

"Beetlejuice, the moment of truth is at hand," Easy said. "At least, for your sake you'd better hope it's the truth."

"Maybe we could talk this over," said Beetle-juice, dangling upside down. "Maybe work out a deal or something."

"No deals," said Easy. "This is bigger than both of us. The public demands you take this test."

"That's what I was afraid of," Beetlejuice said.

"Beetlejuice," Easy explained. "I'm going to ask you some questions. They won't be very hard. All you have to do is answer them truthfully. If you do, I'll quit the race for the presidency. You can be the President of the Neitherworld."

"Not bad," said Beetlejuice. "I like that."

"But," Easy continued, "if you can't tell the truth once, we have decided to banish you for eternity to the Land of the Sandworms."

Beetlejuice swallowed hard.

Easy smiled broadly. "First question," he said. "Do you like Poopsie, the Monster's dog?"

"Great mutt. I love him," Beetlejuice blurted out.

The tendrils shook him violently. They pulled him toward the red bristles at their center and started brushing him across.

"Hey, these are rough," Beetlejuice complained.

The tendrils kept rubbing him. Finally they stopped. They lifted Beetlejuice back into the air. He was suspended for a moment. The arms with the teeth on them wavered slowly in the breeze.

"What's going on?" Beetlejuice wondered aloud.

Suddenly one of the arms whipped up and sank its teeth into his rear.

"Yeeoww!" cried Beetlejuice.

"It's a lie," Easy announced to the pack. A murmur rose in the air.

"This is going to be rougher than I thought," Beetlejuice muttered.

Lydia watched from the Roadhouse door.

"All right," Easy chuckled. "Second question. What do you think of Jacques La Lean?"

"Oh, this is mortifying," Beetlejuice moaned.

Jacques ran forward, eager to hear the response.

"Well," Easy prompted. "Answer the question."

Beetlejuice glared at the red bristles, willing them to believe him. "He's an idiot," he said. "I can't stand him."

Chomp!

"Ouch!" Beetlejuice yelped.

"I knew eet!" Jacques cried. "He likes me. Beetlejuice ees my friend. I always knew he was."

"Well," muttered Beetlejuice. "Maybe the Land of the Sandworms isn't so bad after all."

"That's two lies," Easy said to the crowd. "Two questions and two lies."

The spirits were getting restless.

"All right," Easy continued. "Now for the next question." He considered carefully. "As President of the Neitherworld, do you plan to work hard?"

"This is getting ridiculous," Beetlejuice said.

"Do you?" Easy demanded.

"Yes," Beetlejuice cried. "Yes, of course I will."

Snip went one jaw at his feet. Snap went another.

"Ow, ouch," Beetlejuice whined. Lydia winced in sympathy.

"Another lie," Easy gloated. He laughed smoothly and stepped forward. "Maybe I should make the questions easier," he suggested.

"I don't think it will help," moaned Beetlejuice.

"What color is the sky?" Easy asked.

Gulp, went Beetlejuice. "Green."

Chomp!

Beetlejuice yelped. Lydia shut her eyes.

"What color is the grass?" asked Easy.

Beetlejuice shut his eyes. "Blue," he said.

Snarf! went the jaws.

Beetlejuice howled.

Easy chuckled in triumph. He stepped up close to Beetlejuice and stared him in the eyes. Beetlejuice shrank away. The crowd started chanting. "Sandworms . . . Sandworms . . . Sandworms . . ."

Lydia put her hands over her eyes.

Easy smiled wickedly. "What's your name?" he asked.

Sweat broke out all over Beetlejuice's body. He squirmed in the tendrils, but they held him fast. With all his might he forced his lips together, trying to form a B sound. He had to do it. He had said his name millions of times. He felt his lips pressing together. All he needed to do now was blow some air and he'd make a B sound.

Easy leaned closer. "What is your name?".

Beetlejuice answered, "Lydia."

CHAPTER TEN

THE FINAL JUDGEMENT

"SANDWORMS . . . SANDWORMS . . . SANDWORMS . . . " the crowd chanted loudly. Easy Slider stepped back. Beetlejuice still smarted from the lie detector's last bite. Things couldn't be worse.

Lydia had an idea. It was true that Beetlejuice had vowed not to tell the truth in his campaign. But he had also said he would never lie to her. Which vow was stronger?

"Hold it," she called out.

Easy turned to glare at her. Lydia stepped forward. She approached the lie detector, where Beetlejuice was hanging upside down, wrapped in tendrils.

Lydia laughed nervously. "You're being silly," she told Beetlejuice.

"What are you talking about, Lyds?" Beetlejuice asked. "I'm stuck. I just can't tell the truth."

Lydia raised her voice, so everyone could hear her. "Beetlejuice," she announced. "What is your name?"

"Don't do this to me, Lydia," Beetlejuice said. "It's embarrassing. Not to mention painful," he added, looking at a very vicious set of teeth.

"I want you to answer me," said Lydia loudly. "What is your name?"

"Lyds, babes, I'm begging you," Beetlejuice pleaded. "Don't make me lie again. Just leave me to the Sandworms."

Lydia gave him an angry look. "What's your name?" she demanded.

"Beetlejuice," Beetlejuice cried. "Beetlejuice, Beetlejuice, Beetlejuice." His eyes opened wide with surprise.

The sharp-toothed vines swung through the air, but didn't bite.

"I told the truth," Beetlejuice said. "Wow!"

"Beetlejuice," Lydia asked. "What color is the sky?"

"Blue," Beetlejuice said. "Hey, this is fantastic!"

"What's going on?" cried Easy Slider. "Get this girl out of here."

But the gang was murmuring its approval.

Lydia continued. "What color is the grass?"

"Green," cried Beetlejuice. "The grass is green. I love it! I'm telling the truth."

"Of course you are," Lydia told him. "You know you'd never lie to me."

"Oh yeah," Beetlejuice said. "Why didn't I think of that?"

"No fair!" cried Easy. "This is not fair at all."

"Oh yes it is," Lydia answered him. "You said all Beetlejuice had to do was answer one question honestly. So far he's answered three!"

"I've been tricked," said Easy. "This is no fair. I'm not giving up the campaign."

"Okay," Lydia announced. "One more question and you can go free."

"Shoot," replied a confident Beetlejuice.

"Why should people vote for you for President of the Neitherworld?" asked Lydia.

Beetlejuice thought for a moment. "Hey, Lydia," he said. "Don't ask me that."

"Come on," Lydia prompted.

"Hey, this is no fair," Beetlejuice complained.

"Beetlejuice," said Lydia sternly. "Why should people vote for you?"

Beetlejuice gritted his teeth. "Well, I've learned something during this campaign. I've learned that what's fun for me isn't always fun for someone else. Jacques likes speaking French. Ginger likes tap-dancing. It's true that I lied a bit here and there, but what do you expect? I'm Beetlejuice! I'm sorry for the lies I told. But one thing is true. I never pretended to be anything but myself. Beetlejuice. The Ghost with the Most. I'm not a dignified ghost. But what's more important, dignity or fun? I haven't got all the issues together yet. But hey, this is your afterlife. What issues are there to worry about?"

The ghosts and goblins went wild.

The lie detector lowered its tendrils, setting Beetlejuice back on the ground. Lydia ran up and hugged him. "Thanks, Lyds," Beetlejuice said. "You got me out of a tough spot there."

"What are friends for?" Lydia said.

"Please," Beetlejuice said. "No more questions."

"Byetelzhooze," cried Jacques, running forward. "My friend."

"Oh no," Beetlejuice moaned. "Anything but this."

"Byetelzhooze, ze lie detector proved eet," said Jacques. "Byetelzhooze ees my friend!"

"Face it, Jacques," sneered Beetlejuice. "The lie detector was wrong."

Chomp! went the jaws.

"Yeow," cried Beetlejuice, rubbing his backside. "Get this thing away from me.

Creatures surged forward, surrounding Beetlejuice and Lydia. Beetlejuice was forced to shake hands and talk to the ghouls. Babies were thrust at him, which he kissed and thrust back. Spirits said hello, and patted him on the back.

"What an ordeal," said Beetlejuice, after the crowd had evaporated.

"Hurry," said Lydia. "It's time for the news."

The two of them rushed into the Roadhouse. Beetlejuice switched on the television.

"Hello, folks," came a familiar voice. "This is Dan Splatter with the Six O'Clock Ooze News. Our top story: the Neitherworld gets a president."

"Here it comes," Beetlejuice said.

"Shh," whispered Lydia. "I'm trying to listen."

"Today the Neitherworld held its first Presidential election," said Dan Splatter. "After a long, tough race, Beetlejuice came out the winner."

"I'm the new president!" Beetlejuice sang. "We've got to celebrate."

"Great idea," said Lydia.

"I was thinking about dinner at the Twenty-One Bug Club, or the Four Sleazens. Then we'll head on over to Slimelight for a dance party in my honor. The whole Neitherworld is bound to be celebrating."

Lydia giggled. "Sounds great, Beetlejuice."

Just then there was a knock on the door.

"Who could that be?" Beetlejuice wondered. He walked over to the door and opened it.

"Byetelzhooze," cried Jacques, leaping through the door. "My old friend. Congratulations!"

"Oh, brother!" Beetlejuice moaned. "Not again."

But Jacques wasn't alone. The Monster from Across the Street barged in next. "Beetlejuice!" he bellowed. "Mighty proud of you. So's Poopsie." Poopsie dashed up to Beetlejuice and licked him across the face.

"Ugh," said Beetlejuice, pushing Poopsie away. "Maybe you could feed old Fester Breath here some mouthwash. Like a half a gallon of bleach."

The Monster slapped Beetlejuice on the back. "You're such a kidder," he exclaimed.

"Who's kidding?" Beetlejuice asked.

"Ta-da!" cried Ginger, bounding through the door. "Beetlejuice," she said. "I'm so happy that you became president that I made up a whole new tap dance in your honor."

"Uh-oh," Beetlejuice complained. "Anything but that."

"Yes," cried the triumphant Ginger. "And I'm going to perform it for you right now." She started clattering all eight feet across the floor.

Beetlejuice slapped his hands over his ears. "Help," he moaned. "This can't be happening."

"And since we are such friends, now," said Jacques, "I've decided to be your assistant."

"Just what I need," Beetlejuice mumbled.

Lydia chuckled. "That's what you wanted, Beetlejuice," she said. "People to serve you!"

"Yes," said Jacques. "I've already been hard at work."

"What do you mean?" asked Beetlejuice, bewildered. "I haven't given you anything to do."

"That's right," said Jacques. "So I went out and talked to everyone I could find." He pulled out a huge stack of paper. "Here's a list of all the things people want. Longer nights. Dimmer days. Colder weather . . ."

"Lydia help me!" yelped Beetlejuice.

"Oh, I don't know," laughed Lydia. "Things seem to be under control here. I think I'll be on my way back to my world now."

"Lydia," cried Beetlejuica, giving her a panicked look. "You can't leave. What am I going to do?"

"Sounds like you've got lots to do!" Lydia giggled. Then, saying his name three times, she disappeared.

"Lydia!" Beetlejuice yelled, jumping up and down. "This is no fair. I demand a recount. A shorter term. Easy Slider should be the President. Not me. He's the better slime. Lyds, come on Babe. I'm too young for this. Help! Lydia!"

And when Lydia appeared in Peaceful Pines, for a moment she thought she was still in the Neitherworld.

"Dad," said Lydia, spying on her father. "What's going on?"

Charles put down a towering stack of papers. "These pages explain all the issues that need to be voted on. They've all got to be read by Tuesday."

Lydia was horrified. Leave it to Delia to get Charles mixed up in so much work. "This means you won the election!" Lydia exclaimed.

"No, no," said Charles. "Delia won. She was a write-in candidate. Everyone was so impressed by her they voted for her even though her name wasn't on the ballot."

Just then Delia entered the room. Seeing the stack of paper she shrieked. "This can't be!" she cried. "I can't do all this. I'll never have time for my sculpting. I'll never have time for my life. There's got to be some mistake. Isn't there some way to refuse this honor?"

Lydia laughed and went to her room. Two victories in one day, she thought. And they couldn't have happened to more deserving people!